MW01235239

The Christmas Gift
by
Izzy James

To Judy

thanks for believing in me.

Published by Elizabeth C. Hull
Bent Knee Press
e-book edition: December 2015
First print edition: July 2016
ISBN: 978-0-9852291-5-3

Mom,

This one is for you.
I love you,

~Izaberry

Prologue

"Attention all passengers on Diamond Airlines Flight 3924 to Richmond departing from Gate C15. Our plane is inbound, and as soon as it has landed and we have deplaned, cleaned and serviced it, we will begin boarding. We expect a thirty-five minute delay."

Jack Callahan stretched the kinks out of his back, let out a deep sigh, picked up his backpack, and stood up. He'd been still for too long. Sitting in libraries, standing in museums. His very cells were tired of the inactivity. He was sure he had most of the information he needed for his next book and he knew where to look for answers as the inevitable detail questions came up. His mind was full. It was time to percolate. As soon as he got home, he would head out down the trails and start writing. When he was done, he would do a little painting.

He sat back down in the pleather chair once again waiting as the sun began to set. It's rose-gold light shot through the window and kissed the hair of the woman sitting opposite him. Her hair was the color of wheat. He could capture it with a blend of raw umber and white maybe, but the rose color and the metallic way it reflected, that would be harder. He stared knowing that the sun was moving fast through its setting. He would have only seconds to capture that particular look. He felt for his phone.

He shifted his gaze down to her face.

"Take a picture. It will last longer."

Before she could protest, he snapped the picture and said what he had never said to anyone. "I'm sorry. I'm a painter, and I was captured by the light as it touched your hair."

"Right." Her eyebrows shot up, lips thinned to a frown, eyes darted to the side. She turned ninety degrees to the right to dismiss him, which gave him a further view of her wheat colored hair in the sunlight. It was probably creepy, but he snapped another photo.

Thirty minutes later, he was in his window seat on the plane looking out at the tarmac fading in the dusk.

"I hope you've turned your phone off for takeoff." He snapped around at the sound of her voice. There she was checking her seat number with the label of the seat next to him.

"Would you care to inspect it?" He offered up his phone.

"No, that's quite all right." She plopped down in her seat and tucked her purse into the space beside her. Her book, *The Secret of Gabriel* by Jack Murphy, sat unopened in her hands.

"What kind of things do you paint?"

He told her of the woods around his house and the trails that latticed through them. As he told her about the small animals that inhabited his land, her hazel eyes widened in interest and shifted in color from squirrel brown to gray. When she asked him questions, a slight smile formed on her lips, and the smooth and creamy crepe-like surface of her face crinkled with the memories of her life. He couldn't remember a more beautiful face.

No, beautiful wasn't the word. Comely, no. Fetching, no. Alluring, close. Exquisite.

That was it.

She was exquisite.

"So no people then."

"What do you mean?"

"I mean I asked you what you painted, and you told me about your woods and animals. Do you do portraits of the people you randomly snap in airports?"

"The picture."

"Right."

"No, I don't paint people. But I am often looking at light. I really was caught by the incredible way the light was interacting with the color of your hair." He had to hold his hand back from reaching out to experience the silky, fine texture.

"I can understand that." She dismissed him with a little smile and turned her eyes down to her book. His seat got a little cooler.

It was a statement of fact, yet he could feel her disappointment. Had she been flattered? She wouldn't be if he'd actually painted her. He hadn't told her, his true artistic medium wasn't paint. It was words. He loved words, and picking just the right word could take him hours. He was the best selling author whose book she held in her hands. He turned toward the window. What would she have done if she'd recognized him?

Chapter 1

One Year Later

" Jack Callahan is a pig."

Erica Thomas plopped down in the chair opposite her best friend and business partner Ann Berry. And Ann Berry, her very best friend since high school, sat there and said with a straight face and a twinkle in her eye, "He's a real good looking pig."

Erica rolled her eyes. "Come on, really?"

"Yes. You should know. You met him in the airport, not me."

"Why do I always feel like I'm a school girl when I talk to you?"

"Maybe because we were school girls together? Come on now, you have to admit that Jack Callahan is gorgeous."

Her anger deflated as she felt herself color at the thought of him snapping her picture. The truth was, what she remembered most about their encounter were his descriptions of his home and the paintings he made of the landscapes and animals. She didn't think she would ever forget his clear amber eyes. Her attraction had been so strong that she had retreated back into her book. Strong enough that she still thought about him a year later.

"Ok, he wasn't bad to look at. But you and I both know that that is not enough. A man has to have certain qualities that make him suitable."

"Here we go again." Ann let out a frustrated breath, "Erica Thomas. Love is not a statistic."

"No, it's not. But I am a statistician, and numbers do not lie. Good looking is not a measurable quality, but liking women who are too young for you is. It's an indicator of character. Bad character." Erica stood up and went over to her own desk.

"Ok. Ever since high school you've had this notion of the perfect man. He doesn't exist. But the perfect man for you does."

"Apparently not. Look at me, I'm forty-five years old. I live with my mother. I've never had a serious relationship. I think God decided I didn't need a man." Ok, that wasn't strictly true. She had been serious about Ron Brownly. Ron Brownly had not been serious about her.

"You live with your mother because you want to, not because you need to."

"True, but you get my point. God just didn't have a man for me."

"I don't believe it. You just haven't found him yet." Ann took a sip from the tea cup on her desk. "You have to do this interview. Jack Callahan requested you. By name. He's probably got a new book coming out. Anyway, it's been scheduled for over a week, and it will give us that boost we need in December."

"I wouldn't care if it was anyone else." Erica let out a resigned sigh.

"He's your favorite author, I would've thought you'd be excited."

"That's a loaded statement. You know I never like to meet new people. And he's a famous stranger. And any pleasure I would have taken in meeting him evaporated the minute I found out about his dating requirements." Not that different from the long gone Ron. She'd been dazzled by him. Since then she'd not been dazzled by anyone.

"He's not the only man I ever heard of that likes younger women. At least we can be sure that he's not been mooning over you for the last year...which might be a little creepy."

"True. But have you read his books? How can he have such an understanding of human nature and be so..." She slapped her hand on her thigh.

"Shallow?"

"No, it's not shallow, it's...I don't know yet, but I'll figure it out."

"Well, whatever you do, don't worry. You'll be fine." Ann smiled displaying all the confidence that Erica wished she had.

That was two days ago, and Erica didn't feel any better about the interview as she left Brandywine in the freezing rain on her way to meet Jack Callahan.

Erica had always been the quiet, serious one. In high school, Ann Berry had been a cheerleader, always smiling, always dating. Erica had been studious. After high school, they had gone to the same college. Ann majored in journalism, Erica majored in mathematics. In their late twenties , Ann married Steve Johnson and had three children. Erica took on bigger projects, moving up in her organization.

"Fraud. The word is fraud," Erica Thomas said out loud to herself. She knew Ann had thought that it would be a treat for Erica to interview best selling novelist Jack Callahan, writing as Jack Murphy, author of the Friar Aldred mysteries.

And at first, she'd been delighted about driving the fifty miles to see a real-live successful author. Not just because she liked his books, but because they needed every penny the paper could make. Interviews

3

with a successful local author would expand their readership. Everyone would be interested in reading an article about Jack Murphy. While he wasn't exactly a recluse, he didn't give many interviews. Name recognition, according to Ann, was the name of the game.

Erica's trouble started when she looked him up online in preparation for the interview. His website had one posed photo of a bearded man wearing flannel. Wikipedia had the same photo.

Excitement deepened to intrigued when she realized that Jack Murphy, the author, was Jack Callahan, the painter she had met in the airport a year ago. Would he remember her? Probably not. After all, it was just her hair color that had interested him. But she had not forgotten him. She had even been reading one of his books when she met him. Too bad he was a another typical male just like Ron Brownly. You think they have depth and that they are worth your time and effort only to find out that you're just a notch on their bed posts.

"New York Times best-selling author of mysteries featuring Friar Aldred." She had read elsewhere, "Lives on a secluded farm in the foothills of the Appalachians in Virginia. Never married. Only dates women in their twenties."

Pig.

She guessed it wasn't really any of her business that he preferred younger women. Plenty of men did. Although at age forty-five she had to admit she didn't find twenty-five-year-old boys in the least bit interesting. Not at all. They were too busy playing video games and eating pizza, or, worse yet, stressing over the fat content of their food.

What did those girls see in a man old enough to

4

be their father?

He was good looking. True. When she met him, he had a rugged, outdoorsy look. At the airport, he had been clean-shaven, and had on a blue flannel shirt and a worn brown sack-jacket. Now he had a beard. She had recognized him by his clear, amber-brown eyes.

He had told her he was a painter. Had he lied to maintain his privacy? At the time, she had believed him, but her career had taught her time and again that instincts could be wrong. Not enough data.

Word was, he was hard to interview and kept to a strict script.

Why the young women?

Why did she care? Was she jealous?

Yes.

Jealous of what? He was successful. Well, so was she. Not in the newspaper business yet, but she was a top-notch statistician.

She was happily unmarried. And she didn't want to be married. God had not sent her a man, and she was content as she was. She had no need of companionship with a person who was bound to wish she was someone or something she couldn't be. She was forty-five-years old. She did her hair the way she liked, wore what she wanted to wear, and lived as she pleased. And it was Christmas time, her favorite time of year. The songs, the lights, the promise of redemption, she loved it all. Regretted nothing. She was happy, despite the nervous thrill in her mid-section that bubbled to life every time she thought of Jack Callahan over the past year.

Unable to reconcile her inexplicable attraction to him while still comparing him to certain barnyard quadrupeds, she tried to focus on what she had to ask him. Ann had given her a list of questions. They were typical and boring.

Where do your ideas come from?
How do you deal with writer's block?
What does your typical day look like?

Erica was more interested in the soul of the man who gave Friar Aldred the understanding of the shadows associated with even the most mundane of human behaviors.

What fascinates you about light?

How could the man who gave Friar Aldred his insights only date women in their twenties?

Erica sat up straight and adjusted her black power-suit. The freezing rain had turned to snow, which was melting on contact with the road. She was glad she had thrown her big winter coat, a change of clothes, snow boots, and knitting bag in the back just in case the weather worsened. Preparedness was something she'd learned from so many years on her own. The knitting bag, she had to admit, was just eccentric. Erica hated to be bored. Anywhere she went, she always had two things with her: books and her knitting. Whether she needed them or not, they made her comfortable.

Snow in her part of Virginia was always an uncertainty. This time the weatherman was calling for fifteen inches to fall overnight, but she didn't believe it. There weren't any statistics to back it up that she knew of, but in this part of the state, they only got a good snow every five years or so. That happened last year, so while it wasn't looking very good right now, she expected it would turn right back to rain before her interview was over. A quick glance a the clock confirmed she was right on time as she made the turn down the gravel driveway.

Chapter 2

The long gravel driveway was wooded on both sides. Snow was gathering on the trees. The drone of windshield wipers and beating rain quieted with the soft fall of snow. Thanking God for four-wheel drive, she pulled out of the woods into a large clearing. In the middle sat an enormous two-storied log cabin. On the side, set a good bit way from the house, was a large wood pile.

A man reached down, picked up a log, and placed it on a large wooden stump, raised an ax above his head, and brought it down in a controlled swing. Erica could almost feel the muscles of his shoulders and back flex as he cut through the log in one blow. Leaning on the ax, he reached down, picked up the pieces, and placed them on a the large pile. He turned to face the driveway and began to walk toward her.

This was a *man.*

Her mouth went dry.

She got out of the truck just in time for his arrival.

"Hello," he smiled.

Now I know what they see in him, she thought.

"Erica Thomas." She stuck out her hand. He stepped closer, grasping it. His smile warmed his face but did not soften his sharp amber-brown eyes. He was wary.

The interior of the cabin was still.

It glowed honey-gold and peace. Its warmth contrasted with the view of the cold, gray day framed in floor-to-ceiling windows on all sides of the large rectangular room. The first floor was wide open with a spiral staircase leading up to a second-story loft. In front of the staircase was a massive Christmas tree decorated with large, old-fashioned, multi-colored lights. Erica couldn't help the smile she felt. She loved multi-colored lights. A couple of wrapped packages already waited under the tree.

On her left, the main floor contained a kitchen area set off by a half-wall in one corner. Diagonally across from it, sitting between two large windows was a desk flanked by two tall bookcases. To her right, on the far wall, was a large stone fireplace with a banked fire.

Jack hung her coat on a peg near the door.

"Have a seat." He waved to a long trestle table that was dark and scarred with age. A bench ran along the side she was facing, and chairs were on the opposite side. It looked like a table for a large family.

Erica couldn't take her eyes off of him as he moved through the room toward the fireplace to place a log on the embers. The way he moved jarred her with its controlled smoothness. It reminded her of a powerful, well-oiled machine. He could probably pick her up and carry her wherever he had a mind to. She pushed away the image that thought brought to mind.

"Something to drink?" he asked as he crossed the room towards the kitchen.

She placed her notebook and purse on the table and stepped over the bench. "I'd love a cup of tea."

"Tea it is."

She fished out her tape recorder, pen, and notebook and put her purse on the floor. She heard a K-cup machine bubble out its hot water. Looking up, she saw two portraits hanging on the partition. It was then she noticed that the walls were bare of paintings.

In fact, nothing hung on the walls at all. Curious for a painter. Surely the walls should be covered with his art works. She spun around to take a look at the book shelves. She was a little far away to read all the titles, but she didn't see copies of his bestsellers there either. Turning back toward the kitchen, she studied the two portraits.

They were both the same size. One was of a couple walking hand in hand along a forest trail. Their love was as obvious as the sunlight illuminating the leaves. The way they leaned into one another, they almost appeared to be two sides of the same person. The artist had used the same colors on each of the figures accenting different hues in each individual. The effect made them one.

The second painting was of the same couple with a child. The child also shared the colors of the parents, but the colors were sharper, more vivid. Lovely was the word that came to mind. Erica felt an old longing rise in her heart. A family of her own would have been nice. But her life had been good. God had not chosen a man for her. She had had a career. A wonderful, fulfilling career as a statistician, and she wouldn't have changed a minute of the challenges and triumphs she had experienced. These feelings were just coming with retirement.

Had he painted the portraits? He'd told her he didn't paint people.

Her concentration was broken when he came around the wall from the kitchen carrying a tray with two mugs, a sugar bowl, a jar of honey, and a small container of cream. She turned to face him, expecting him to sit across the table from her with his back to the lovely portraits. Instead, he carried the tray to her side of the table and straddled the bench next to her.

Legs open, left elbow on the table.

"How was your drive?" he asked as he unloaded the tray.

Erica was struck by his scent when she turned to face him. He smelled of woods and snow. His eyes glowed a golden amber like the wooden room around them. Closely cut brown hair framed his face, a light stubble covered his chin. He was close enough that she could run her hands up his thighs.

"It was fine." She stammered while she worked on reining in her thoughts. "The snow was coming down pretty hard at times, but the roads were clear, so I kept going."

"When I saw the forecast, I wasn't sure you'd come."

"Oh, well. Weather forecasts are not very reliable. I was surprised you agreed to the interview."

His eyebrows raised. He blew on his coffee.

"Every article I've read about you talks about your reluctance to do interviews." And the young girls you date, she thought to herself, trying to get a grip on her reaction to him.

"I'm a private person." He smiled and blew on his coffee again.

"Exactly. Why does such a private person wish to write best-selling books and invite the scrutiny of the world?"

"It's not the best-selling part that interests me. It's the conversation."

"Like you shouldn't complain if you didn't vote kinda thing?"

"Not exactly." The corner of his mouth crinkled in a half smile. "There's a conversation going on between a writer and a reader," he gestured outward, "and larger than that, the community of readers is conversing with the culture at large."

Here was the man she had seen in his books.

"We are such a small paper that I was just surprised."

"How did you come to be working for a small-town paper? You don't strike me as a newspaper woman."

"That's a long story." She took a sip of her tea, "I hear that you have a strict list of things you won't talk about."

His eyes darted up from his cup.

"I am a private person. I don't have an actual list per se, but if there is something I don't wish to answer, I will not answer." His voice was quiet and strong, like man who is used to the quiet might be. Like man used to being heard the first time he spoke might be. "My only stipulation is that I see the article before it's published. I've been burned by newspapers before."

"So why did you agree to this interview?" she asked again.

"I believe in helping local businesses."

"I'm at least fifty miles from here."

"Close enough."

She accepted that as she new she must. He clearly wasn't going to elaborate, but she didn't believe it. It just didn't ring true, but it didn't really matter because he was a fraud. Her hands shook as she flipped the page in her notebook to buy herself some time. She tried to write a note, but it looked like a child playing at writing. It didn't matter; she wouldn't ever forget a second of this interview.

"Did you paint those?" She pointed her pen toward the paintings on the wall.

His eyebrows shot up again.

She'd caught him off guard. She took a silent breath.

After a long moment, he said, "I did."

"I thought you didn't paint people."

His eyes warmed in recognition as he smiled and shook his head. "I did say that," he paused, "These are the only people I've painted. They are my parents."

"It looks like you have a talent for portraiture."

"Not really." He looked down.

"Why don't you paint them? People I mean?"

"I don't like what I see in them. I painted my parents because I like them. Having them in front of me reminds me to pray for them."

Pray for them?

"A picture would do that."

"A picture is just a snapshot. A blink in time. A painting takes time and knowledge. It captures the soul. So you see a picture can't remind me of what I see when I see them." He paused and searched her eyes.

Her heart skidded a beat. She took refuge in Ann's list of questions.

"What do you do when you have writer's block?" She blazed with embarrassment, "that is, if you ever get writer's block. Do you get writer's block?"

Two cups of tea and two hours later, Erica had enough to write her article. Reluctantly, she closed her notebook. Jack Callahan had intrigued her with his talk of painting and his parents. She didn't want to leave. She wanted to stay and sit in front of the fire and learn more about him.

"I guess that's it. I appreciate the time you gave me today." Erica stuck out her hand for a friendly handshake. The instant her hand touched his large one, the power went out. She'd been so absorbed in the conversation she had not taken notice of the hour or the snow. The light from the windows, now even more prominent with the indoor lights out, glowed a dim gray. Snow dusted the sills, coming down so heavily that she couldn't see farther than a few feet.

"I'd better get going." She put her notebook in her purse and headed for her coat on the peg. He followed close behind and held her coat for her as she put it on. The brush of his hand at her hairline sent delicious tendrils of desire through her body.

At least she assumed it was desire. She didn't exactly have the right dataset of experience to be sure.

Chapter 3

Jack Callahan was jubilant when he came outside with Erica and found the snow piled up on her truck. He nearly shouted for joy when he saw the huge tree that had come down across his driveway.

"Thank God for four-wheel drive. I'm so glad I brought my snow boots," Erica said, gingerly stepping down the porch steps in her high-heeled shoes. He grabbed her elbow when she slid and kept a hold as she made her way across the driveway.

"Boots are good. Did you bring any other clothes?" She looked up at him sharply, a question in her hazel eyes. He pointed down the driveway toward the tree in response. "Looks like you will have to stay here for a bit."

"Dang." was all she said as she made her way to her truck. Once there, she took off her formal coat, threw it in the backseat, sat down on the drivers seat and began to change her shoes. "How long do you think it will take to clear that tree?"

Jack looked down the driveway. "Can't tell from here. I'll have to take a look. Care to join me?"

"Yes." She reached back into the truck, and retrieved her cell phone from the charger, and put it in her pocket. Then she pulled on her winter coat.

He had no need to hold her arm as they walked down the driveway together. More's the pity, he thought to himself. Jack had hoped he would find out more about her during the interview, but she was sharp and kept the conversation focused on him. He'd revealed more about himself than he'd intended. But then again, maybe that's what it was going to take.

He hadn't been able to forget her in the year since they had met at the airport. It had to be providence that he had seen her picture in the byline of that little newspaper. He wanted to know her better, and if it took feeling a little vulnerable, he was willing to give it try.

Jack judged the tree to be about two feet in diameter. Most of the large trunk lay across his driveway. What had been the upper branches lay sprawled across the power line that ran adjacent to the driveway.

"What do you think?"

"I think you won't get out of here before tomorrow. I can't start on this until the power company deals with the downed power lines. My chainsaw is in the shop, so I will have to borrow one. After that it will just take a couple of hours."

He could see her battling for control of her emotions. She clearly did not want to stay with him. She turned and started back up the driveway dialing her cellphone. He followed a respectful distance behind.

"It's me. You won't believe this. Nothing about this has gone right. I'm stuck here." Her voice was controlled frustration. "One of his trees came down across his driveway onto a power line." She turned and looked back at him. He nodded and sped up to pass her as he headed into the house. "Stop laughing. It's not funny." Was the last thing he heard.

"I'm sorry I can't help it," Ann giggled at her. "I mean really, what're the odds that you of all people would get stuck at Jack Callahan's house in a snow storm?" More giggles erupted.

"Ann, my mother is alone at home."

"Oh, for heavens sake. Don't worry about your mom. Steve and I will check on her. Besides, you know your mom. She'll will want to take care of us. She's not afraid of anything."

"Maybe I can get a cab."

"There are no cabs out there. Steve and I tried that once, but it's too rural for those. Besides, the roads are probably too bad. They're saying it's the worst storm in a decade, and the overnight lows are supposed to be in the teens. You may be stuck for a couple of days."

"I can't be stuck for a couple of days. I don't have any clothes...I'm just...I don't want to do this."

"It'll be all right."

"Yeah."

She hung up and called her mother to let her know the situation.

"We still have power here, Honey. So don't worry. Is he cute?"

Erica slapped the phone to her chest, looked around for Jack, and then put the phone back up to her ear. "Mom."

"Listen, Erica, stay where you are. You shouldn't be out on the roads. Didn't you see the forecast? It's going to be really icy, and you don't need to be on those roads until they clear up. I know what you think about forecasts, but this time I think they may have gotten it right."

"Yes. I. Know. Ok, well I'll call you tomorrow and update you."

Great. She should have known that everyone would think that being snowed in with Jack Callahan would be a dream come true. Well, it wasn't her dream, yet here she was stuck in a house with a man she was really beginning to like whom she knew she should distrust. Great. Well at least she had her electronic book reader. She took her bags, clothes, and knitting out of the truck. Have Book, Will Travel, she thought as she headed up the steps.

Chapter 4

When Erica walked back into the cabin, she was engulfed in the smell of frying onions. Jack had rekindled the fire, and the room was regaining its golden glow from the flames.

He came out from the kitchen.

"You are welcome to stay here with me," he smiled, "I thought we could have stew."

"Thank you. It smells good." Was all she could think of to say. It felt awkward now that the interview was over and he was the famous Jack Murphy and she was regular Erica Thomas stuck in the snow.

"I think I'll go change if you will point me in the right direction." The bathroom was a generous size, yet, like the rest of the house, it was sparsely decorated.

It was such a relief to be out of her suit. Years of wearing them day after day had not made them any more comfortable. That was one benefit of retirement. She wore what she wanted to. Blue jeans, a cotton knit top, and a thick pullover sweater fit exactly how she felt. She would have liked to be _Flashdance_ chic in her sweater, but she never did manage that. The image in the mirror confirmed that she still hadn't. Nope, it was just plain, old (emphasis on old) Erica in a sweater. At least she was comfortable.

She followed the dinner smells and stood at the edge of the galley kitchen looking in. Jack stood in front of a six-burner gas stove. He had a large dutch oven on a back burner.

"I thought I would go for a walk if you don't mind."

He dumped a pile of meat into the pot and turned the stove off before putting the pot in the oven. "Not at all. I'll come with you. I thought I would check in on a couple of my neighbors."

It was not what she'd had in mind, but anything would beat sitting around in the house trying to figure out something to talk about. Besides, it would give her a chance to see what his neighbors thought of Jack Callahan, not that it really mattered. She'd talked to people about Ron Brownly too, but she had been young and relied on the opinions of the other young women she worked with. What a mistake. Of course Jack Callahan was not the corrupt the son of a corrupt local politician. No. He talked about his readers with the bigness of soul that she thought she would find in him.

Chapter 5

Jack walked her down a barely visible trail toward a clear break in the woods away from the house. The snow was above her ankles but she had no difficulty in her boots. The landscape was a feathery gray and white. The silence soothed her anxiety.

In the woods, the light from overhead was darkened due to the trees, but the ground was lighter from the snow. She could see what felt like miles.

"So how did you come to work for a small-town newspaper?"

Erica pondered for a minute how to answer. She didn't want to like Jack Callahan. Being attracted to him was one thing; liking him was another.

"When I retired, I decided to go into business with my friend Ann. She owned the paper, but she was looking for a partner. So after I retired, I bought in." She emphasized the word "retired".

"Retired, huh?" He smiled again. "What from?"

"I'm a statistician."

"Oh" Take that, Mr. I-only-date-women-in-their-twenties.

"You must be very smart."

"Yes, I am."

He laughed at that. His was a wonderful, full-bodied laugh that made her laugh too.

"Sorry."

"What for?"

"Well, it was a bit over the top."

"No, it's the truth. I knew it the first time I met you. What did you do with stats?"

"I worked in logistics. Most people start to yawn

about now."

"I can see that, but I would think that it's not the logistics that are interesting, but the types of problems you solve and the techniques you use to solve them."

She stopped in her tracks. How had he seen that?

"I guess that's what makes you a best selling author."

"What do you mean?"

"You're ability to see into people and understand their point of view."

"Perhaps." Then he stopped and turned, "We are just about there. I have a favor to ask. My neighbors don't know who I am. I mean, they know me, but they don't know I'm Jack Murphy, and I'd like to keep it that way."

"Privacy."

"Yes."

"Ok."

Standing about two hundred yards from them was a small white farmhouse. Smoke chuffed out of the chimney, but the windows were dark. Erica walked beside Jack across the field to the back door.

Jack opened the screen door. His body filled the doorway. His knock was muted by his leather gloves. Snow dusted his brown hair. His lips were stiff with the cold.

"I knew it'd be you, Jack. God bless you for coming on such a day." The old man's face rippled back into a toothy smile. "Come on in. Fire's going in the livin' room." He reached out a hand to Jack. As they shook hands, the old man saw Erica. "Sorry, Ma'am. I didn't see you standing back there."

Jack stepped into the kitchen. "Ben, I'd like you to meet Erica Thomas from Brandywine."

Erica smiled as she stepped into the kitchen and

stuck our her hand. "Nice to meet you."

"Welcome!" Ben stepped forward to clasp her hand in both of his. "Now, may I offer you both a cup of coffee? I was just having one myself. That's the good thing about a gas stove. They still work when the power's out." He waved toward the stove with an old camp percolator sitting on the burner. The remnants of a sandwich lay on a cutting board next to the stove.

The kitchen was a large rectangle with cranberry red tile a and white metal cabinets. Erica could almost hear the echoes of children shouting and laughing.

"We can't stay. I wanted to check in and make sure you have everything you need. It's gonna get cold tonight."

"I heard that, but between the two of us, I think I've got enough wood by the door. The fire is hot. I got some blankets for the sofa. I'm good."

"Got enough candles?"

"Yep, I'm good. You know, I've lived here all my life, and I'm not worried about a little power outage. The Lord made this day too. Amen?" His eyes twinkled at them.

"Amen. Listen you call if you need anything. I'll be right over. Of course you know you can come over to my house."

"I know it, I know it, but I'll be fine." Then he turned his cheerful countenance to Erica, "How about you, Miss Erica? Are you fine? What brings you out in this weather?"

Erica explained about the tree and the downed power line that had stranded her at Jack's.

"Well, the Lord couldn't have provided a better host for you if you have to be stranded."

"Yes, he has been most kind."

"Well, I would be surprised if he was otherwise."

Jack looked down at his boots. "Ok, Ben, we're gonna go. I want to check in on Jenny before we head back."

"Yes, you better get going. It'll be dark soon, and you don't want to be wanderin' around after dark in this mess. Give my love to Jenny and the kids."

"I will."

They trudged through deepening snow another mile or so until they saw another farmhouse set back from the road. A weak stream of smoke trickled from the fireplace chimney. Erica could hear children laughing. This time Jack led them to the front of the house.

A beautiful woman with long blonde hair answered the door. She was almost six feet tall with clear blue eyes. She was dressed in blue jeans and a shabby sweatshirt that on her looked chic. Erica's muscles clenched.

"Hi, Jenny."

In one smooth motion, Jenny stepped out onto the porch and put her arms around Jack.

"I'm so glad you came." She stepped back and waved him inside, "I'm having trouble with the fire. Can you take a look? My boys are so excited for the snow."

Erica stepped in behind Jack. "Hi, I'm Jenny." Jenny offered her hand to Erica. "These are my boys." She waved toward four small boys jumping up and down for Jack's attention by hollering, "Mr. Jack! Mr Jack!"

Erica's tightness eased, and she found herself smiling at Jenny. "Erica."

"They love snow, but I haven't quite got the hang

of fires yet. Jack has been teaching me, but this is the first time I've had to try on my own. We're from Florida."

It was a large room with big windows and little else. The walls were empty.

"I know it's bare. I'm just waiting until the kids are older. I don't want them to get hurt, so the end tables and other stuff are in storage."

"Oh, I just assumed children would learn to get around furniture."

"Do you have children?"

"No."

"Oh." Jenny turned her attention to Jack who was working on the fire with two the smallest boys hanging on his back. "Can you fix it?"

Jack carefully stood catching one boy as he slid around Jack's side while the other slid to the floor landing on his feet.

"That should do it. Just keep adding wood. You'll need to watch it tonight to keep it going, unless you and the boys would like to camp out at my house."

Jenny looked from Jack to Erica and back to Jack. "No, me and the boys are going to have some hot chocolate and read some books."

"Are you sure?"

"Yes. We'll be fine."

"I'll be back tomorrow. Call if you need anything."

"Thanks I will."

They walked back in silence down the narrow trail. Jealousy was foreign to her, and she knew she had absolutely no right to feel that way after one afternoon's visit, yet there it was. Of course there was a beautiful woman around. Why wouldn't there be a beautiful woman around Jack Callahan?

They ate dinner across from each other this time at the table. Erica sat in a chair so he could see his parents.

Midway through the meal, she wished she had sat on the bench side so she would have something to look at besides him. She liked him more and more by the minute. Why was that? And why did he keep looking at her like that? There were no sunbeams shining on her hair now.

"Where are your parents?" She asked between mouthfuls of stew.

"At home."

"Oh, so they're not gone."

"Nope. They live a couple of miles from here."

"So close? I got the impression they were either dead or a long way away."

He smiled in response, "Nope. They are close by. I called them while you were on the phone outside, they're at home, threatening to take an excursion in their sleigh."

"A sleigh? Like pulled by a horse?"

"Yes. My dad loves horses, and my mom loves sleigh rides. But they probably won't venture out until tomorrow after the snow stops."

She smiled at him, but she was afraid it only came out as a stretching of her lips and not the smile she intended it to be. Ugh. This was so awkward. She wished she could disappear into her book.

How was she going to be able to read another Jack Murphy book? Now that she had met him, *really* met, him she knew she would never feel the same about his books.

"There's no sex in your books," she blurted out

before she could stop herself.

His eyes shot up.

"I mean there are no sex scenes at all. I mean you talk about sensuality and stuff, but there's no sex. How do you get away with that? How did I not notice that before?"

He started to laugh. He laughed and laughed till she saw little tears forming at the corners of his eyes.

She looked down. Abrupt and abrasive does it again. She picked up her bowl and took it to the kitchen.

"I'm sorry," she said when she returned to the table, "Sometimes what I think falls right out of my mouth. I should never have said that." He wiped his eyes as the last tickles of laughter quieted down.

"You are right. There are no sex scenes in my books because I think the conversation is bigger than that. I'm not interested in other peoples bedrooms. I'm only interested in mine." He caught her square in the face with his eyes focused on hers.

All the thoughts she had flew out of her head at that moment. Was it an invitation? Surely not. She was too old for him. Besides, what would he do if he found out that she had never participated in that particular activity? Wouldn't he laugh if he knew she had waited for a marriage that had never happened? After what felt like an hour, but was probably fifteen seconds, she bent down and retrieved her purse so she could find her reader. For some reason, she felt comforted having it in her hand. And then she sat down because as her brain was reviving, she realized the intellectual aspect of the argument he presented. She was interested in that.

"Tell me more about this conversation you keep talking about."

He pushed his bowl away and rested his arms on the table. "Each book or story presents an argument...an idea that must be reckoned with not just with the characters but with the reader...there are millions of conversations going on all the time on different levels with millions of people.." He gestured widely including the whole world. "Lots of people talk about sex because its fun, it's lusty...and it's ok...but it's not the only thing to talk about..."

"I thought you were going to say something like you didn't believe it was right or something like that."

"Oh, no. I believe in sex." He chuckled then, but it was an inclusive laugh that he assumed she would understand.

"Ok, but I have another question for you."

He looked open, eyes twinkling.

"There are things missing here." She waved toward the room behind him.

"What do you mean?"

"It's what I don't see. Where are the paintings? Where are your books? Your walls are bare."

With that, he rose from the table.

"Come with me. I want to show you something."

Chapter 6

Outside of her ever-present discomfort with new people and crowds, Erica was always annoyed that her introversion kept her from noticing her surroundings at times when her emotions ran high, like when she was going to take a walk in the woods with Jack Callahan.

How else could she explain that had she missed the small building at the back of the house? They must have walked right by it on their way to the woods.

It was another beautiful cabin, about three quarters the size of the main house with just one story. It too had lots of floor-to-ceiling windows to let in the light.

The sun was long gone from the sky. It was cold and still snowing. Erica snuggled into her down coat. Jack swept the snow away with his booted foot, opened the door and stepped into the room. Erica followed.

The room was dark and still and cold. The absence of wind provided relief, but no warmth as the glowing fire in the house had. Erica could hear him moving about the room. With the scrape of a Zippo, a candle flared to life. He lit an oil lamp from the flame and then lit several others that cast a ruddy radiance upon the room.

Erica felt time slip away as she gazed around her. It was a wooden work room. It smelled of wood and paint and mineral spirits. A controlled chaos compared to the starkness of the house. Paintings were stacked along the walls and were tacked to the supporting beams. There were cans of paint brushes set on wooden shelves that also held paints in tubes and small pots. Cloths smeared with color hung from various hooks. It was gloriously alive with images of all types of plants and animals. A reverent scrapbook of snapshots of a soul engaging with the world around him and the souls of the those he engaged looked back out at him.

Each looked like a snapshot of a conversation. Animals, trees, flowers, sky different scribblings of color. If Kincaid was the painter of light, then Callahan was the painter of the soul. The details of the eyes and poses were all precisely drawn. In the imperfect candle light, they gave the appearance of being just a shimmer away from life. If she caught them out of the corner of her eye, they would spring to life and run. They were like his book characters: precisely drawn; captured for an eternal instant.

A canvas sat upon an easel placed at the center of a bank of windows that constituted the back wall of the room. A canvas tarp draped over the whole thing hid whatever he was working on. In front of the covered easel was a barstool that had been nailed to a makeshift dolly. Off to the right, on the floor, was the beginning of a painting of a tree.

Jack stood in the middle of the room watching Erica's face as she moved from section to section. Her expression flowed from watchfulness to wonderment to reverence. His heart expanded to fill his entire chest cavity and threatened to squeeze out of his thickened throat. He looked down at her feet, waiting for her to finish, struggling to control his impulse to pick her up in his arms.

When Erica stopped moving about, she walked back over to stand in front of him. He looked up from her feet to her eyes. His vulnerability slammed into her heart. She warmed and searched for words that would let him know she would never betray the trust he had placed in her by allowing her access to this room.

"What do you think?"

"I can see why you don't paint people," she pointed to small sketch of a fox. "It's as though he stopped to talk to you. No guile or malice."

His gaze didn't leave her face as he approached her.

"You are the most exquisite woman. . . ."

She rolled her eyes. "Right." He caught her chin just as she began to move and placed his lips on hers in a single soft kiss. He kissed her again, and she responded before she knew what she was doing, pressing herself into the warmth of his body. As he deepened the kiss, Erica felt his hand slide under her coat around to her back. Slowly his hand moved back toward her waist and up toward her breast. Her knees buckled.

"Stop," she said and stepped back.

Jack stepped back, hands in the air, and turned away. "I'm sorry."

Erica could think of nothing to say. She was not sorry, but it was not ok. The warmth of his body was still imprinted on hers. She felt lost in the coolness now invading her coat. She could feel herself falling for Jack Callahan, and that was not going to happen. It wasn't the first time a pig had come on to her. She might be a virgin, but that didn't mean she had never been pursued. But this was the first time she'd ever been in danger of falling for the pack of lies of a womanizer.

Exquisite indeed.

How often had she told her clients that analysis is required because humans are not good at interpreting data without some formalized structure? Something outside of themselves so they could make sound decisions. She needed space and time so she could remember crucial things about his character like . . . She drew a blank.

"I need to get out of here."

Chapter 7

Once in the house, she paced.

Pacing in her own house was routine. When she got upset, she put her energy to good use by getting out the cleaning supplies, and she'd go to town on her house, talking to herself all the while until the upset was gone. It was a good system, but she was not at home. She was here in Jack Callahan's spotless house. And she was ashamed and angry.

How dare he kiss her like that? And more to the point: how dare she like it like that? She swung around for another pass and remembered the dishes. She removed her pullover and headed for the kitchen bringing a lit oil lamp with her. Here was another anomaly: why didn't someone as successful as Jack Callahan have a generator?

As she looked under the sink for some dish soap, she remembered her husband model. It was just what she needed. She tried the tap and found they still had running water. She put a little water in the sink and searched through her mind for the nodes of the model she'd built in graduate school. She would have to put it down on paper to properly work through it, but she thought she could remember the basic structure.

The idea had first come to her when she was in high school watching some sitcom in which the mentor character told the mentee that finding the right girl was easy. One just needed to make a list. She had spent days creating her list.

In graduate school, she'd needed something for a project, so she adapted her earlier list into a probabilistic classifier. She had been older then and discarded silly requirements like tall and dark, for more reasonable qualities like honest, kind, and faithful. It was just the thing she needed now to work through the contradictions she was finding in Jack Callahan. Once she was done with the dishes, she would dig out her notebook and get to work.

Chapter 8

"Damn it." Jack kicked the chair on its dolly sending it careening into a wooden pillar. Kissing her had clearly been a misstep. It didn't matter that he had wanted to since that day in the airport.

Her response to his most hidden self had intoxicated him.

"Well what did she think would happen?" he said to the chair as he returned it to its rightful place in front of his canvas.

Of course that didn't matter. What mattered was the commitment he'd made five years ago. Erica was the first real challenge he had faced since then. Perhaps that was always the case with the woman you meant to marry. He would have to ask Ben about that.

He lifted the cloth and took a look at his progress. It was good. His fingers itched to pick up a brush, and he knew he had to give her a few minutes to think, but the light wasn't right and it was too cold. He would have to go inside soon. The temperature was supposed to fall into the teens overnight. They would need to stay by the fire to keep warm. She was going to really like that.

He grinned. He liked her spunk.

Spunk? No, spirit. He liked her spirit. He had never met anyone like her, and if today was any indicator, he was going to enjoy every minute of getting to know her better.

He turned the knob forcefully to announce his entry into the room. He had an inkling that she would be angry. He didn't want to add to the conflagration by startling her.

She was seated on the couch in front of the fire, bent over writing something when he opened the door. She didn't respond to his presence, so he couldn't tell if she was ignoring him or just absorbed in whatever it was she was doing. Choosing to believe it was the latter, he moved quietly upstairs to retrieve blankets and some sweats for her to sleep in.

Erica released her grip on the pen she'd been using as soon as she heard Jack's footsteps on the stairs. She reordered her things so that he could not see the model she was working on when he returned.

"Are you working on your article?"

"You may be able to avoid the elephant in the room, but I am not that kind of person."

Jack's eyes widened and his lips tightened. He looked down, and when he looked back at her, he had relaxed his features. He rubbed the palms of his hands together.

"An apology is in order." He cleared his throat. "Erica, I am very sorry to have stepped over the bounds of propriety. I will not do so again. You have my word that I will not touch you again tonight."

Erica frowned, "Did you think I wouldn't catch that?"

Jack's eyebrows went up, and a gleam lit his eye. "Do you mean that I did not apologize for kissing you?"

"Yes, and you've only promised for tonight."

"I am not sorry for kissing you. I have wanted to kiss you since the moment I saw you a year ago, and it's gotten worse since you arrived this afternoon. And since you will likely be leaving in the morning I only need to promise for one night."

His words slapped all the words right out of her head . . . . again.

"I've had a brilliant idea while I was digging out these blankets. How about we decorate the tree this evening?"

"Um, sure," was all she could muster. Had he been thinking about her since their airport encounter too? Nah, he wasn't that kind of guy. Or was he?

"I'll be right back." She nodded in agreement and plopped down on the couch. Had she been wrong about him? Certainly Pastor Ben liked him. And Jenny and the boys did as well.

He returned with a large cardboard box and placed it on the floor. He left again, this time for garage and returned with a handful of candles and saucers. He placed the candles on the saucers and set them on the steps to illuminate the tree. Then he went to the kitchen and returned with popcorn and a popcorn popper for the fireplace. These he set down on the hearth. He disappeared once more and came back with two glasses of iced tea.

"I would make hot chocolate, but I thought we could do that later after we decorate the tree.

"Iced tea is fine."

"I have these little traditions when I put up my tree. Usually I play some Christmas music, pop popcorn, and have a little cocoa."

"You do this by yourself."

"Some years I have, yes. Other years, my parents come over. This year you are here."

He stepped over to the box and pulled the flaps open. Glitter sparkled from the opening.

"I love Christmas. Don't you?" he asked as he pulled the first ornament from the box.

Erica relaxed. She could figure it all out later.

For tonight, he'd said he wouldn't touch her, and oddly enough, for some illogical reason, she believed him. "Yes, I do. It's my favorite time of the year. I would say we could play Christmas songs on my phone, but I need to keep it charged in case my mother calls."

His eyes lit up again, "Great idea. We can use my phone."

He retrieved it from his desk drawer and set it on the steps next to a candle.Bing Crosby filled the room crooning, "I'm dreaming of a white Christmas..." Peace eased into Erica's spirit. Everything and everyone would be ok for one night while she decorated this tree and thought of the Savior who came one night as a tiny child.

Chapter 9

"Are you awake?" Quiet as a breath, the question startled her. Jack was laying on his back in his sleeping bag, one arm under his head, looking at her. She was snuggled down under two blankets on the couch in front of the fire. Flames illuminated the room casting warm shadows.

"Yes." She whispered back. It reminded her of sleepovers at Ann's house. Ann's parents had strict rules about bedtimes. Erica's mother never did. It was more magical somehow to stay up late talking at Ann's.

"Want some cocoa or something?"

"Can't you sleep?" Erica yawned. She had drifted to consciousness for some reason she didn't know or care about and felt herself drifting back toward sleep. The temperature in the room made her dream of heat maps. Radiating rings of heat emanating from the fire diminished in warmth as they battled the chill in the room. Erica, on the couch, was on the cusp of the boundary ring. Cold at the back, warm at the front. She didn't want to get out of the the blankets. Besides she didn't like the idea of being awake with Jack Callahan in the middle of the night. Her response to his kiss was unmistakeable. If he did it again she didn't know if she could say no.

"I seem to be awake for now."

"Well, if you're gonna make it anyway, I'll have some"

Jack responded by wriggling out of his sleeping bag and walking toward the kitchen. Erica stayed nestled down, listening to his movements, drifting in and out of a dreamy fantasy where she did not say no.

The kitchen floor was an iceberg even through his socks. Jack didn't know why he was awake, but he was glad Erica had wakened too. He stirred the hot chocolate, once again thankful that his mother had talked him into the big gas stove. A cook he was not, and he wasn't ever going to be, but when his mother had heard he had decided against a whole house generator--the type he had insisted should be installed in his parents house--she advised him to get a gas stove. "If the power's out, you gotta be able to boil water," she had argued. He had conceded because it made her happy. This hot chocolate was not the first time he was glad he had listened to her.

Nighttime. Erica in the nighttime was almost more than he could resist. But interestingly enough, his faith was why he would respect her conviction. That didn't make it easy. She wasn't going to react well if he moved too fast, and he was ready to ask her now. But she was probably right to take things slow. He had waited this long. He would just have to wait a few more days, which could really be broken down into hours. He took a deep breath, stretched out his arms, and did a couple of jumping jacks to tamp down the hum of electricity lighting his brain with possibilities. He poured the cocoa into mugs and headed toward the living room. Too bad he wasn't very good at waiting.

She was still groggy when he handed her a mug.

"It's hot." He winced as she tried to resettle herself into a sitting position while balancing the cup. He grabbed it just in time to avoid a scalding. After she was situated, he handed it back.

He wanted to sit on the end of the couch, but

chose an adjacent chair instead.

She looked at him over the steaming cup. She was lovely. Yes, lovely was the word. Her hair mussed from sleep, her eyes and skin smoothed by rest, illuminated by flames. He reached for his sleeping bag and draped it over his lap.

"I love your house. Did you build it?"

"Yep. About ten years ago."

"It's nice that your parents are close by." It was a stilted beginning, but that was ok. It was his turn. Nighttime was a time for confidences, and he was going to ask the questions.

"Tell me about your parents." She smiled at him. It was not a sarcastic grimace, which she used often in conversation with him. This time it was a genuine smile full of warmth. "I was just thinking of them."

Her parents met in college and were married immediately thereafter. Her father was a mathematician and her mother was a lawyer.

"My father died when I was five. My mother has told me since then that she has had her love, and she will see him again when she goes home."

"So she hasn't dated since his death?" Really? Of course he had heard of that, but given the last five years of his chosen life of celibacy, he knew it couldn't have been easy to live that long without your love. Would he do that if Erica was taken from him?

"I think she may have gone on one or two, with our family physician after his wife died, and maybe when she was much younger. But if she did, nothing ever took."

"It couldn't have been easy," fell out of his mouth before he could capture it.

"I don't know. I've never been married."

"Never?"

40

"Nope. God just never sent the right one. And I was always so busy with work. Time seems to have slipped away from me. I'm forty-five. Never married. No children."

"Does it bother you?"

"No." She blew on her hot chocolate and took a sip. He waited. "Sometimes. You know about being successful. It takes a lot of time. I enjoyed my job," she looked into the fire.

"But?" he prompted

"But I see my friend Ann with her children and I do wish sometimes that I had made some time for that. That God had sent a man for me to marry." She blushed as she looked at him quickly and turned back toward the fire. He held onto the arms of the chair to restrain himself from vaulting over the chair to give her all the children she wanted. " When I retired, I came home to live with my mom. She seems so frail to me now. I don't want her to go home yet." Tears welled up in the corner of her eyes. He moved to sit on the floor in front of the couch and took her free hand. "She's all I've got."

It was too soon to tell her what he believed had been revealed to his heart, so he sat and held her hand quietly knowing that she would not be alone, not as long as he was alive.

Chapter 10

Erica opened her eyes to see Jack with his back to her standing in front of the fireplace. Ann Berry was right: he was "a real good looking pig". Only, she was beginning to wonder about the pig part. The good looking part was confirmed every time she looked at him.

This morning his broad shoulders were covered in a green plaid flannel shirt that tapered into a well worn pair of jeans.

Who knew that stocking feet could be so intimate?

He squatted down to adjust the fire, one arm resting on his knee. There was something in his hard masculinity that made her feel safe. He had been up about every two hours or so all night tending the fire. She could imagine that he would do that for his family. Heck, for that matter, he would do that for whoever it was that he found himself stranded with including Paster Ben and Jenny and her four boys. Last night, though, he had done it for her. She snuggled deeper into the couch. She was comfortable and she didn't want to move.

Erica sat straight up at the sound of jingling bells. She kicked her feet free of blankets and swung her legs around from the couch to the floor. Jack was still squatting in front of the fire. His sleeping bag lay rumpled off to the side. The door flew open with a whoosh of cold air.

"Good morning!" An older woman came in carrying a cast iron dutch oven with two hands. "I brought cinnamon buns!" Erica's stomach growled.

She stood, picked up her blanket and held it to her midsection.

Behind the woman stood a taller, older version of Jack Callahan, carrying a large quilted satchel full of yarn and knitting needles.

His parents. What will they think?

"Hey!" Jack rose from the fire, took the dutch oven and placed it on a table by the couch, spread his arms wide, and hugged both of them.

Call Mom.

"You must be Erica." The woman extended her hand, "I am Bonnie Callahan, Jack's mother. This is Red." Erica dropped the blanket and extended her hand. Bonnie hugged Erica's handshake in her two hands.

"Nice to meetcha." Red beamed.

"Jack told us you got stuck in the snow. Thank God you weren't on your way home and got stuck out there somewhere on the way to Brandywine. It was a nasty storm last night." Erica relaxed at the concern in Bonnie's soft gray eyes.

"Yes, thank you."

"How about some coffee?" Jack crossed through the small circle with the cinnamon buns and headed toward the kitchen. Jack's parents followed. Erica folded the blankets and stacked them along with pillows on a chair. Grabbed her purse and headed to the bathroom.

She pulled out her phone and sent her mother a text.

"Howz it going?"

"Good. Power still on. Praise God. Are you on your way?"

"No. Power still out. Will check on powerline and let you know."

"Heard 50,000 people without power. It could take days."

"Great."

"Hang in there."

"Love ya."

"Love you too, honey."

Great. She didn't need to worry about her mother. Now she just needed to worry about herself falling for the very unsuitable Jack Callahan. Laughter at the table pulled on the corners of her mouth. Memories of their shared laughter last night tugged at her heart. She had avoided asking him about younger women and more importantly what he had meant about wanting to kiss her since he met her at the airport. She hadn't wanted to spoil the fun of decorating the tree, or the intimacy of the hot chocolate shared in the night. Her abruptness had messed up more than one holiday she could remember. More laughter drifted through the door. They seemed to be such good people. Jack liked his parents.

Did she like her mother?

Yes. Yes, she did. She always had enjoyed their time together. Her mother would share stories of her cases and Erica would tell of her analysis. They shared their faith, too. Yes, Erica liked her mother and looked forward to telling her so when she got home. She smiled when she pictured her mother safe and sound at home with the power on, nice and warm.

After she had told Jack about her mother, she had felt a calming peace drift into her soul. She had not shared those feelings with anyone. Jack had then told her of his meeting Pastor Ben and how that meeting had led to his faith. They had fallen asleep just before dawn.

That peace had not left her, and as she listened to

the laughter at the table, she wondered if perhaps she had been wrong about Jack Callahan. Maybe her judgement had been too quick and too harsh. He definitely wasn't Ron Brownly. Jack lacked the slimy selfishness that Ron was slathered in.

Was Ann right? Could the heart be trusted to provide input to such a decision? Her head always ruled, and she had always succeeded in every area but one. Had she missed something? Could Jack Callahan be the man that God had for her?

He appeared to be ranking pretty well in her model on all the major points. He was kind, generous, respectful, and he loved his mother. Of course social models are terribly subjective, but they do help a body think through a problem. And of course she hadn't had time to really do any calculations. She would have to do that when she could be alone with her computer. But in a purely qualitative way, he was doing pretty well. Could he be the man she had waited for?

Erica washed her face, and ran fingers through her hair, put it up in a Scrunchy she kept in her purse for that purpose, and went out to join them.

"We saved some for you." Jack offered her the plate of oversized pastries. Her mouth watered, and she wondered if it would be rude to have two. While she carefully selected one bun, Jack placed a large mug of tea at her elbow.

"Dad and I are going to check on Pastor Ben and Jenny."

"I thought you and I could stay here where it's warm." Bonnie smiled at Erica.

"Sure." It would give her some time away from Jack to clear her head, and maybe she could work on Diana's Christmas sweater. It wasn't going to knit

45

itself.

The men left directly after breakfast, and Erica and Bonnie settled down in front of the fire to knit. Erica pulled out Diana's sweater and began to knit the rows. She was working in the round and found her rhythm quickly. Bonnie was rummaging through her enormous bag.

"So, how did you meet Jack?"

Erica looked up from her needles. It was abrupt, but then she was known for abruptness herself.

"Actually I just came to interview him for the Brandywine paper. I should have left earlier, I probably could have gotten home, but the tree fell across the driveway. I still would have left except for the downed power line."

"For some reason, I thought you knew him before that."

Erica looked up again, truly startled this time. Why would she know about that?

"Well, technically I did meet him about a year ago in an airport, but it wasn't a real meeting. I didn't even know his name. We just had one of those airport conversations that strangers sometimes have."

"I love the colors you chose for that sweater." Bonnie pointed to the sweater forming on Erica's needles.

"Thanks. Nothing compared to Jack. His studio is amazing."

"It took him a year to build it."

"Really?"

"It had to be right for the light. Don't know where he gets it from. Red and I are like wooden decoys when it comes to art."

"I don't know about that. The colors of your husbands sweater and your own match in a nonobvious way."

"You noticed that."

Erica smiled in return. She wondered if Jack's painting inspired the color matching of his parents or if Bonnie's color choices inspired Jack's painting. She would have to ask Jack.

The rest of time that Jack and Red were gone, Bonnie recounted to Erica numerous stories of Jack's four older sisters and their children. Erica was fascinated. She'd had no idea that Jack had any family outside of his parents. From the paintings, she'd assumed he was an only child.

"We saw power trucks on our way back. We should have power soon." Red blasted into the room with a rush of cold air. Erica allowed her needles to relax on her lap. She was relieved the workman were in the area but she wasn't sure she wanted to go just yet.

She had to settle this feeling she had before she left. Suppose she had been wrong about Jack Callahan? Suppose he had been telling the truth that he had not forgotten her in a year. It was worth it to find out even if it did make her uncomfortable for another evening. And really, all data analysis requires data. She definitely needed more data.

Bonnie and Red stayed for lunch and then prepared to set out for home in their sleigh.

"I bet your fire is out. Are you sure you don't want to stay here?" Erica asked as Jack went for their coats.

"I'm sure it's out, but it doesn't matter. We have a generator." Bonnie smiled back at her. "Don't worry about us, Red knows what he's doing." Jack came back with coats, and together they walked the older couple out to the sleigh.

"Jack insisted we have a generator when he built the house. I told him he should have one, too."

"I don't need it," Jack said quietly.

"So he says. It's been so nice to meet you, Erica. I'm looking forward to seeing you again soon." Bonnie gave her a little hug.

Erica didn't know how to respond to that. She had no reason to see Mrs. Callahan again soon. "It was nice to meet you, too." Was all she could muster, but it was heartfelt. She really did like Bonnie Callahan and it would be wonderful to see her again someday should their paths cross.

After waving them off, Jack led Erica toward the garage.

The driveway was piled high with snow, but the sky was clear.

"Wanna help me shovel the driveway?"

"Oh, yes. I'm tired of sitting."

Erica looked down the long path toward the road. She was, in fact, glad of the opportunity for some exercise, but she didn't think she wanted to work quite that hard.

"You shovel all that?"

"No, I use the tractor down there, but it's better to shovel up here by the house."

"Where do we start."

Jack grinned and handed her a bright orange snow shovel.

It had been cold enough that the snow was fluffy and easy to move. The kind that wouldn't hold together well for a snowball. They had cleared the first section near the house and were heading to where the driveway near the house blended toward the long section he used the tractor for when the first snowball flew.

Erica answered in kind, and so it took them two hours to shovel what should have taken twenty minutes. Jack spent another hour or so scraping the snow from the driveway using his tractor. Erica used that time to take a shower and organize her things. The power should be on soon and she wanted to be ready.

Jack fixed leftover stew for dinner, and they sat on the floor on Jack's sleeping bag in front of the fire. He filled her in on his visit with Jenny and Pastor Ben.

Jenny had finally mastered the fireplace, and the boys had made two large snowmen in the yard. Pastor Ben was praising God.

After they had eaten, silence fell between them as they once again found themselves gazing into the fire.

Erica could not remember ever feeling this way with another person. It was right to sit here with him like this on a snowy night in front of a fire. The quietness she felt was peaceful despite his nearness. She hated to disturb it, but she knew she must. This would be her last night here, and she had to know before she left what to think of him.

"How do you handle two such gifts? Do you struggle between them?"

"I see them as two facets of the same gift. In order to write, I have to describe; in order to describe, I have to see; in order to see, I paint."

Erica thought about his paintings and the beautifully drawn characters and she could see the correlation.

"I need to ask you about last night," she continued.

"What about it?"

"When you said that your weren't sorry..."

"I'm not sorry that I kissed you."

"No, the other part..."

"That I have wanted to since I met you?"

"Yes. Did you mean that?"

He searched her eyes. "What is your real question?"

"Why did you request me to come interview you?" She looked down at her hands, and twisted the garnet ring on the middle finger of her right hand.

"Because I have followed your pieces in the Brandywine paper. I like your honesty, and I share your point of view."

He picked up her hand and held it in his own and she let him. His hand was twice the size of hers, dry and warm.

"I'm abrupt."

"Yes." She looked at their hands entwined. The desire she felt whenever he was near flamed to the surface.

"I know you probably think I'm old fashioned, and maybe I am, but I'm ok with that. It's what I believe."

"I'm ok with that."

With his free hand, he reached up and put his arm around her, and she let him do that too. She fit into his shoulder just right.

"Tell me more about your mom, you said you live with her."

"Well I do now. Last year...right after I met you actually, she was in a bad car accident..she got a terrible concussion." She sat up and turned to face him, "I had already been toying with the idea of retiring and when the offers came around I took it. There was just something about seeing her there so fragile...it struck me..she was alone with her law practice and I was alone too...might as well be together." She turned in his arms and pointed at him. "Your turn. Has your mom always dressed them like that?"

"Yes. She thinks she's not an artist, but her eye for color is razor sharp, like perfect pitch."

He held out his arms, and she rested back in his embrace. It was perfect. The fire, Jack's arms, ... She hated to do it, but she had to ask. Tension tightened her stomach.

"I have another question."

"Anything."

"Younger women?"

Jack's lips hardened into a line as he pulled away from and turned to face her. Erica's stomach twisted into a knot, and the warm glow of the evening slipped up the fireplace.

"What about younger women?"

"Even though you keep your phone in the desk, you have to know of the reports that you only date younger women. Much younger women."

"What is your point?"

"My point is that you and I have been . . .,"she faltered like a schoolgirl. "I don't know how to say it, but we have been . . . " The words stuck in her throat. "And how can you be interested in girls so much younger than you? I thought you had such depth of soul..." There. She'd said it, not as descriptively as she did with Ann, but he knew what she meant.

"You're a snob." He turned from her to face the fire.

Erica gasped out loud.

"No. I'm. Not. I simply asked a question. What is a fifty-five year old man doing with a twenty-five-year-old girls?" Her eyes widened, "Never mind...I don't want to know." She got up from the blanket and realized she had no where to go.

"What makes you think that a twenty-five-year-old woman has only her body to offer?"

"What are you talking about? I have worked with twenty-five-year-old boys. What in the world could they offer me?"

"So young women are stupid and worthless?"

"I didn't say that."

"I bet you were remarkable at twenty-five."

"What has that got to do with anything?"

"Erica, my life has changed in the last five years. I haven't dated anyone in that time."

"I'm not a snob, I'm a statistician. You like what you like and you have always liked. I am not that. Just because you gave your life to Jesus, why would that mean that you no longer prefer younger women? You could find yourself a younger Christian woman."

She had said it. She could never be that twenty-five-year-old again. She was forty-five. Her heart wrenched with the wish that she could turn back the clock. But the truth was the truth, and she wasn't going to give up everything that she was to be something she couldn't be to get something that would compromise her principles and eventually make them both miserable.

With that, she picked up her blanket and began to prepare her bed on the couch keeping her back to him.

"Are you the only one who can commit to something bigger?"

"Is an older woman supposed to be the sacrifice that you give to God? No, thanks." She said quietly and crawled under the covers keeping her back to the fire. She had nothing more to say, she'd wanted more data, and she'd gotten it. He liked younger women, and he would always like them. He defended his liking of them. It would only lead to trouble. Thank God this had gone no further. She was so close.

Chapter 11

Erica woke about eight o'clock the following morning to the vision of Jack's back as he tended the fire. The quiet in the room was no longer peaceful. She sat up and began to fold her blanket. Jack turned, and before he could speak, the power came on. The house began to hum as the electricity flowed through bringing life back to normal.

Erica put her feet in her boots, got on her coat and went to inspect the driveway.

She heard Jack crunching down behind her. Halfway down she could see that the workman had cleared the tree from the driveway, leaving large rounds of wood on either side. Erica turned and headed back to the house for her things. She passed Jack without saying a word.

A car pulled into the driveway as she reached the steps. She turned in time to see a short, brunette in her mid-twenties get out of the car and step into Jack's arms.

Erica looked around the room once more to forever store the memories and gather her belongings. She didn't have much: her purse, satchel, and briefcase. Her briefcase seemed heavier than usual. Must be time to clean it out. She could get to that later. One more look, one deep breath, and she stepped once again onto the porch. Then she walked to her truck and loaded the passenger side with her stuff.

"Erica!" Jack's voice was cheerful. Great. She turned to see Jack and the girl standing side by side with Jack's hand resting lightly on her upper arm.

"This is Mindy. My assistant." He dropped his hand.

Erica put on her professional go-to-meeting face. Her lips stretched into a rubber smile while her arm extended into a handshake. "Hi. Erica Thomas. Nice to meet you, but I've really got to go." She turned to Jack and offered her hand. "Ann will be in touch about the article. Thank you for your time and hospitality."

Jack took her hand and once again searched her eyes. "I look forward to hearing from you." This time the amber pierced her heart.

She turned from him, gave a little wave, and stepped up into the drivers seat.

"Bye," she called cheerfully and drove down the driveway. She stopped long enough at the end of the driveway to send an *"I'm on my way"* text to her mother before pulling on to the main thoroughfare.

The roads had been treated but the icy patches that remained claimed her concentration all the way home.

Chapter 12

Erica felt her eyes relax as she took in the familiar objects of home. She slumped into her favorite chair. Her mother occupied it's mate in front of the fire.

"Oh. Mom"

"Hello, Raccaberry"

Yes, she did like her mom.

"How are the roads?"

"Ummm, ok. Why?"

"Well, I'm a little dizzy, and I think we might need to go to the doctor."

"A little dizzy?" Erica's heart strained. If her mother hit her head again, she could have permanent brain damage.

"I fell down."

"And you didn't call me?"

"I got your text, and I knew you would be here soon. So now you are here. Let's go see Charlie. My coat's in the closet."

Erica retrieved her mother's coat and waited while she got to her feet. She reached out with both hands, and her mother took them as she weaved from side to side. Erica then let go of one hand and turned toward the door. Her mom put both hands on Erica's left arm. They walked forward together. They had taken ten steps when Erica grabbed her mother from veering off into the wall. Acid rose in her throat. She could not hit her head again. If Jack were here, he could carry her to the truck safely even across the snow and ice.

Don't even go there she told herself.

"How long has this been going on?" Erica asked

once they were safely belted into the truck.

"It started this morning. I was going to call June to come and get me when I got your text. Charlie couldn't see me until now anyway, so it worked out." With that her mother sat back in the seat and closed her eyes.

Charlie Morgan had been the Thomas physician since before Erica was born. Her mother had been friends with Charlie for years. Erica had entertained the thought that he and her mother might get together a few years ago when Charlie's wife had died. Her mother had set her straight on that score quite clearly at the time.

"Not even tempted," she'd said in no uncertain terms. She'd had her love, and Charlie Morgan was not it.

"Didn't you tell me when you met Dad that God told you he was the one."

"Yes."

"Did He tell Dad too?"

"If He did, your Father wasn't listening. He was a mathematician you know. He thought everything was by the numbers." She reached out and took Erica's hand. "Like someone else I know."

Yeah, well, the numbers were right most of the time. That's why she liked them. They didn't lie, and they did't care how old she was. She could add them up and multiply them, and it didn't matter if she wasn't twenty-five. In fact, nowadays she could do more with numbers than she could when she was twenty-five.

Erin Lewis came out from behind her desk as soon as they entered the office.

"Mrs. Thomas," Erin put out her hands to assist, "we've been waiting for you. Come with me."

"Hello, Erin. Thanks for getting me in today."

Erin's eyes showed concern and her smile was warm. "No problem, Mrs. Thomas. We can't have you falling down." She smiled at Erica. "I hope it's something simple."

"Me too." Erica replied and sat down next to her mother while Erin got her vital signs. As Erica watched she was struck by how powerful this young woman's care for her mother was. It was not the first time Erica felt warmed by the other woman's compassion for her mother. Erin's clear concern for her mother helped Erica carry her own fear. They were in this together, even if it was only for an hour.

"Dr. Morgan will be right with you." Erin smiled and left the door ajar as she exited the examination room. Erica watched Erin sit down at her desk and begin to fill syringes with insulin while an elderly man seated in the chair next to her looked on.

"I appreciate you doing this for me, Erin," the elderly man said, "these eyes just ain't what they used to be."

She is worthy came a small voice.

"No problem. I'm glad to do it. How's your son doing? Got any plans for Christmas?" Erica continued to watch the scene until Dr. Morgan came in and closed the door.

Chapter 13

Charlie Morgan diagnosed her mom with an ear infection. Erica was too overjoyed to think. It was not the result of the concussion. She drove them to the pharmacy, picked up the antibiotics, and then drove them home.

It was Friday night. Once they were home, Erica put her briefcase in her office deciding that tomorrow was soon enough to tackle the article. She pulled out her knitting and spent the evening with her mom watching their favorite movies and working on Diana's sweater.

Walking her mother to bed was not the ordeal that she experienced earlier in the day. Once her mother was in bed, the night loomed cold and empty in front of her. She had never felt that way about the night before. Usually she fell into bed exhausted from full days. But this day had been different. The past two days had changed her life. Even she did't need a model for that. She had fallen in love with Jack Callahan. She would never be the same again.

She went to her office, and there on her bookshelf she found every one of Jack's books lined up in chronological order. She took the first two down. If she couldn't be with Jack, and she couldn't, there was no mistaking that. Then she could read his words.

Monday morning Erica arrived late to the office. Ann was sitting at her desk and stood up when Erica came in and walked over to Erica's desk.

"Hey, sorry I'm late, I waited for June to come before I left."

"How's she doing?"

"The dizziness is almost gone, but I don't want to leave her alone just yet. She'll probably be fine by tomorrow."

Ann closed her eyes and took a deep breath. "We need to talk."

Ann's face was as serious as Erica had ever seen it in the forty years they had been friends. Erica put her purse and briefcase down and sat down in her chair. She rested her arms on the desktop, hands clasped together waiting to hear the terrible news.

"What's wrong." Erica asked.

"I feel so bad. When Jack called for the interview-"

"You mean when you called to ask him for an interview?"

"No. He called me and asked if we would like an interview-"

"Doesn't-," Ann put up her hand. Erica shut up.

"He said his new book was coming out and wondered if we would like an interview."

Erica stayed quiet, her amazement growing. They hadn't talked about his new book.

"Of course I said yes. We will draw more readers with the article, and we can always use the revenue, especially true at this time of year." Erica felt exasperation rise. She knew all this.

"Yes. But what is wrong?"

"I had no idea that you would get trapped at his house for two days, and the more I thought of you out there all alone, the worse I felt. I looked him up, and you were right. He is a pig."

Erica stood up. "Is that all?" Ann was nearly crying. Erica wrapped her in a hug. "For crying out loud, I thought you were gonna tell me you had cancer or something."

"Don't be silly. I haven't even been to the doctor."

"Well, Jack Callahan is not a pig." Erica sat back down at her desk while Ann perched on its top.

"Is he as good looking at the pictures?"

"Better." At least she could admit that without any pangs. Jack Callahan was the best looking man she had ever seen and she suspected he was the best looking man she ever would see, if her heart had anything to say about it.

"I told him you would send him a copy of the article when it's ready."

"Me?"

"Yes."

"What happened."

Erica's cell phone buzzed on her desktop.

Jack's name flashed at her.

She turned it upside down.

"What happened." Ann looked at the cell phone.

"Nothing I really want to talk about."

"You know that won't work, don't you?" Erica reached into her briefcase and pulled out her computer and her notebook that was opened to the model she had worked on the first night at Jack's.

"That was him wasn't it?"

"Yes."

"You like him and you don't like it one bit."

Erica groaned in frustration. "Why do you say stuff like that?"

"Because somethings are not decided in your head. Somethings you have to use your spirit for and heart too." She slid off the desk. "Your spirit should have more weight than those other things you have on your list." She pointed at the model.

"Numbers don't lie." And they don't care how old you are. She booted up her computer. Her phone buzzed a notification of a voice mail. It was from Jack Callahan.

She was torn. Her fingers itched to tap the button and hear what he had to say. Just to hear his voice would be a blessing. She had fallen for him, but it wasn't going to work, no matter what Ann said or anyone else.

She hit delete.

Chapter 14

By Wednesday she had the article ready and passed off to Ann. It was three weeks until Christmas. The time passed a minute at a time as she searched for things to occupy her mind. Fortunately, Brandywine was abuzz with the season. She kept busy writing articles on everything from the craft fair at the Brandywine Recreational Center to the Brandywine High School Band fundraiser. In her off time, she re-read everyone of Jack's books slowly, seeing for the first time his sense of humor in finely crafted phrases. Each description made her remember the way he painted. The way he smiled. The feel of her hand in his. Reading his books wasn't making her feel any better. In fact, the opposite was true. She felt closer to him while she read his words.

The following weekend, she was out covering the High School Band fundraiser. The band director, Leo Bryant, was a young man in his late twenties, who was continually putting the high school band on the local as well as national map. He was in his second year at the high school and the band was already nationally placed. This summer he made headlines when the band played the opening of the first-ever department store in Brandywine.

Apparently his idea this Christmas was to create a jazzy ensemble out of the band kids and have them play Christmas carols while patrons shopped at the new department store. It was genius. Once again, Erica wanted to ask the less obvious question: "Why?" Why would you, Leo Bryant, an innovative young musician, come to teach, of all things, in little

Brandywine? Brandywine. A village so small it isn't even a rest stop on the road to anywhere. Why?

Carols greeted her when she walked through the large double doors of the department store. There set off to one side were five band kids with Leo Bryant dressed like a gig for Blues Alley in the middle of them. They were sitting on folding metal chairs with music stands in front of those who wanted them. Smiles greeted them as people rushed by with full shopping carts and baskets. Her heart lightened for the first time since she'd left Jack's. It was delightful. She waited for a break to introduce herself. Leo instructed the band to play "Jingle Bells" and stepped away to answer her questions.

"This is a great idea. What made you think of it?"

"Thanks." He kept his right hand in motion for the band, looking over at them periodically to keep them in time. "Old movies. I don't think I've ever seen a Christmas movie that didn't have a band playing on the street or somewhere."

Erica smiled at him. "It's awesome that you noticed that."

He smiled back. "Thanks. It's also good for the musicians to play in front of people. And these," he waved around the room, "are their people." He was a nice looking man when he smiled. If he wasn't so young . . . . She felt herself flame with embarrassment.

"Tell me what you are fundraising for."

Erica took notes while he told her about the cost of the yearly band trip. Any child who participated in the fundraiser would receive a portion of the proceeds to offset the cost of the trip.

That was it. The interview was over. She

thanked him for his time. Leo turned to go back to his students, but she couldn't help herself.

"Just one more question." He stopped and turned back toward her, "Off the record, if you don't mind."

"Sure."

"Why? Why do you teach music in Brandywine?"

He looked a little surprised and turned fully toward her. "Because kids matter. I grew up in a small town, went to school in a large city. It's these kids out here that are the back bone. They deserve the best."

"And you are the best?" She smiled at him. Was she flirting?

"Maybe not THE best, but I'm damn good. And they deserve it."

This guy was not a boy. He probably never wondered about the fat content of his food. He was a man. And a nice looking man at that.

She offered her hand, and he took it, smiling into her eyes.

"Thanks for your time," she said.

"Thanks for coming." He smiled at her again. She felt a small bubble of guilt at her reaction to him.

Just inside the department store was a small sub shop. Erica walked over bought a half a sandwich and sat at a bistro table to hear more of the band and watch its director.

"Well Praise God! Look who it is." Her spirits lifted when she saw Pastor Ben standing there with his tray, sparkling with joy. "Hello, young lady."

"I'm glad to see you," she said when he had settled himself up on the high chair. He began to unwrap his sandwich and without looking up said, "He's doing fine."

Her lifted spirits got nervous.

"What do you mean?"

"You can't stand in the river of life and not pick up a few splashes of knowledge as you walk along. I don't have time to hunt around the bushes."

"I'm not sure I understand what you mean."

"I think you do. You know what I always tell my church? If you have a problem with me that's fine. Some of them do. Amen?"

She nodded with a smile.

"If you have a problem with me, then tell me." He pointed to himself. "If you have a problem with someone to take it directly to them. It's the only way."

"I did that."

"I know you did, and he was wrong about that." He opened his bag of chips and dumped them out on the sandwich paper.

"He talked to you."

"He often does." He munched a chip. "It's pride. I told him that, and I'm telling you. I have something else for you, too. Jesus changes lives. His presence changes the desires of our heart."

"I don't know what to do."

"I think you do." He smiled at her again and took a big bite of his sandwich. "I love that old hymn" he said as the band started to play "Oh Come, Oh Come Emmanuel". They turned to listen while they ate.

Pastor Ben was wrapping up the papers on his tray, "You know he thinks I don't know who he is." He chuckled at that and took a sip of his drink.

"I do know that. He's very private about it."

"He's private about his family, too. His niece Mindy is a beautiful young lady."

Wrong pipes. The drink tickled her lungs as she tried to cough up the soda. Great.

"It's not about that," she managed while wiping the tears from her eyes.

"He called me a snob." It wasn't about that either, but it was the first thing that came to mind. And it had hurt.

"Are you a snob?"

"No. At least I don't think so. I've been thinking about it, and he was right, I wasn't just a pretty face at twenty-five."

"I bet you were." She smiled at the compliment.

"My point is this. By one definition or another, we have all had racy pasts. It doesn't have to define our future. He risked his privacy for you. I've never seen him do that before." He took on a somber tone, his smile gone, his eyes serious.

"I would never betray him in that way."

"I know you won't, young lady. I know you won't." He got down off the chair and opened his arms. "I hug people."

She stepped into his arms and felt comforted. "Well, this has been a treat. I had a feeling the Lord had work for me today." His face brightened again into a big, wide smile. "Merry Christmas young lady. I'll be seeing ya." He took his tray over to the garbage can and left.

It was nice to find out that the young woman was his niece. But it didn't really matter did it? Not to the main argument. There was no reason why his tastes should change, if he preferred younger women he could just as well find himself a young Christian woman who would make him happy. It was logical. Tigers don't change their stripes and men like what they like. It was just too bad it made her miserable.

Chapter 15

Two weeks before Christmas her mother was feeling well enough to get the Christmas tree. Erica was still feeling faded and brown from her visit with Jack. She hoped that participating in their annual Christmas traditions would raise her spirits as they had done the week before when the high school students played.

Both she and Lacey always insisted on a live tree from Svenson's. A light, wet snow was falling as they left the house. She loved it. It was good to be home. She hadn't realized how much she had missed being home while she was gone.

It seemed now that every time she turned around, she bumped into some memory or tradition that had been part of the pleasant rhythm of life in Brandywine. None of the small traditions the town had meant more to her than those of the Christmas season.

They had always gotten their Christmas tree at the same place. In fact, the only clear memory she had of her father was of him tying a tree on top of the car in the parking lot of Svensen's.

Erica had just removed her key from the ignition when her phone sounded a text message alert. She read it as it flashed. It was from Jack.

"Check your briefcase."

Odd. Perhaps he was missing something that he thought might have gotten put in there by mistake or something? Anyway, it didn't matter. If it was an emergency, he would have told Ann as they discussed the article. So it would have to wait until she got home. She wasn't going to let it get in the way of her holiday with her mom.

It was bad enough that she felt mopey most of the time when she would normally be jumping around with excitement. This was exactly why she couldn't be involved with him anyway. At some point, he would realize his mistake and go and find a younger, prettier woman and then where would she be? Alone and miserable. This small bit of miserable was bound to be easier to get over than the large batch of miserable she would have to endure if she was to be married to him for years before he decided he didn't want her anymore. No, this was the right choice, and in time, she would feel better.

Once inside she was a little girl again. The awe she felt at the miracle of Christmas was rekindled by the fresh smell of evergreen infused with cinnamon and apple. A toy train that occasionally sounded a smoky whistle clattered around a track at the top of the room. Bin's lined the walls filled with handcrafted ornaments. In the far corner, cookies and cider sat on a table. The small cabin room was packed with people jostling each other to get a better look at the myriad items for sale.

Elspeth Svensen came in behind and around them carrying a white tree tag. She handed it off to her daughter behind the cash register and quickly turned to hug Lacey.

"Welcome you two. I was wondering if I was going to have to bring a tree to your house!"

They laughed and headed back outside to pick out a tree. Erica held her mother's hand as they made their way around the muddy rows looking at each tree that might do. They made short work of it by choosing the third one Elspeth pulled out of the line for their inspection.

Elspeth's son-in-law loaded the tree into the back of her SUV while Lacey went back inside to grab a couple of poinsettias and a cup of cider.

After getting the tree, they treated themselves to lunch at the Mountain View Pub. The snow had turned to a light drizzle. They sat at the window watching it come down as they drank tea and shared a piece of pumpkin pie.

"I have something to tell you." Lacey began. She didn't look up; she just stirred her tea. Erica felt her stomach tighten. Her mother always started tough conversations this way. It had been the preface to untold numbers of hard decisions. We don't have enough money to send you to ___(fill in the blank). We are not going to ___ (fill in the blank) after all.

"What is it?"

"I've decided to get married again."

"Oh." Erica stuck a smile on her face while she scrounged around her brain to figure out who this man could be. She'd been home for a year and wasn't aware of her mother dating anyone.

"Stop that. You look silly." Lacey began to laugh, giggle really.

"Who is it?" Lacey looked around the room.

"It's still a secret."

"Mom. Does he know?"

"No." Her face widened and her eyes twinkled. She hunched in to whisper. "You want to know who it is?" Erica smiled in spite of herself.

"Of course I do."

"Well, I'm not telling you here."

"Mom."

"Ok." She leaned in even closer and mouthed rather than whispered, "Charlie Morgan."

Erica sat back in her chair, lungs deflated.

"You are not." Her mother twinkled from her seat.

"Ok. I'm not. But why shouldn't I? What do I lose if I do?"

"Only you can answer that."

"What is your answer?"

Confusion. Her brain boggled. This was about Jack?

"Are you asking me why I don't 'go for it'?"

"Yes. You are the one always talking about risk. So talk to me. What do you risk if you marry this man."

"Let's go." It was too public a place. She didn't want everyone to hear her scream.

Erica's heart slowed down, and reason returned as she paid the bill. They walked carefully to the truck hand in hand. Inside the truck was silent except for the wipers squeaking across the windshield at timed intervals.

"Are you going to tell me what happened?"

"Nothing physical happened if that's what you mean."

"You are a grown woman, I'm not asking you that."

"I think I fell in love with a man that I shouldn't have. It all happened too fast."

"I fell in love with your father the first time I laid eyes on him." Erica pulled into the driveway. Her mother went into the house while Erica got the tree out of the truck. She opened the garage, took out the stand, and put the tree in it. Her mother came out to hold the tree while Erica tightened the stand's screws. Once it was secure, Erica carried the tree into the living room where they had staged boxes of Christmas ornaments. They sat down to take a breather and enjoy the sight and smell of the tree.

"I thought the Lord told you he was the one."

"Yes, but that just let me know I was on the right track." Lacey placed a box of ornaments on the table. Erica stood up and started weaving the string of multi-colored lights among the branches.

"That was the spirit telling you that your heart was right."

"Yes."

"How did you know that he would be happy with you forever?"

"I didn't. I knew I would be happy with him. He had to choose what would make him happy."

Erica had thought of that, but when her mother actually said it out loud, it didn't sound like a rationalization.

"He has always gone out with much younger women."

"So. Plenty of men look at one thing and settle down with another. You have to allow that people can change if they want to."

Once the lights were on, they worked in silence hanging the ornaments stopping only to remind each other of the significance of special ones. Then they threaded tinsel lightly on the branches. When they were finally finished, they each got a bowl of chili from the crock pot, and sat on the couch amid the scattered boxes, and ate.

Erica leaned over and whispered in her mother's ear, "I'm still a virgin."

"This worries you?"

"Yes. Wouldn't it worry you? I'm forty-five years old. He'll think I'm a freak . . . . if we ever get that far, that is."

"I think he'll be delighted."

"Why?"

"Because you had the strength to wait until it was right." She paused. "Is he the right one?"

"I have never felt this way about anyone, so he could be. But I messed it up pretty badly."

"Then you will have to pray, and then fix it as best you can."

"I'm not sure how to do that."

"You'll know when the time comes. Next time he calls you might answer the phone."

The text.

Erica pulled out her phone.

"Check your briefcase."

She went to her office and rummaged through her briefcase. And there, wedged between several folders, was a spiral bound book. *The Challenge of Friar Aldred* by Jack Murphy. She ran back to the living room with her hands shaking.

"Look at this." She showed her mother the cover, but did not let the book out of her hands.

"Is that a galley?"

"Don't know. Whatever it's called, this is the next Friar Aldred novel. It's not out yet." She hugged it to her chest.

"I'm going to take a nap while you read it," Lacey said as she got up and headed out of the room.

"Should I?" Her mother turned to face her.

"You think it climbed in there on it's own?"

No, it hadn't climbed in there on it's own, but why did he put it there? Erica sat down on the couch and looked at the book. The cover was a plain, pale yellow, creased from use. She opened the front cover and found a note that he had written:

Erica,

Would I ask too much of you to read my new book? I would very much like to discuss it with you over Christmas. Until then, I'll be too busy working to do much of anything else. Are you free for a few hours at Christmas?

--Jack

When had he written this? Before or after they had argued?

Check your briefcase, he would hardly have written that if he didn't mean for her to read it. Well, of course she would read it. No one in their right mind would turn down such an opportunity. But Christmas was another matter all together. She would have to think about just what that meant later.

She sat and read into the night, stopping only for necessary things like tea and cookies. After midnight, she moved into her bed to finish the last few chapters. Her mother slept till morning.

Chapter 16

Erica stood in front of Lew's Hot Dogs on the corner of Main and Mistletoe watching the snow come down. *How is it that snow and cold make me feel so festive?* She wondered as she shivered with cold and anticipation of the day. As she walked toward the *Brandywine Register* the excitement of the whole village hummed around her. Christmas Eve was tonight, and all the shops were open early for the annual Christmas open house up and down Main Street. Carols spilled out of the shops mingling with the snow as she made her way down Main Street.

Christmas decorations lighten even a shop-fronted newspaper office. Ann had arrived early. The Christmas open house was in full swing. Spiced cider scented the room. A large angel tree loaded with presents sat in the window. Free copies of a booklet of Christmas carols was melting away along with all the Christmas cookies that Ann, Erica, and their mothers had made. Leo and the high school jazz band was playing in a corner. A large clump of mistletoe hung from the archway at the back of the office.

Erica refreshed the stack of Christmas carol booklets. They'd long ago run through the six dozen cookies. Snow was dusting the sidewalks outside. The bell tinkled, and cold wind tickled her neck when the door opened. She didn't look up or turn around but righted the booklets set ajar by the wind. She picked up the empty box, scanned the table, and headed to the back room. She could pick up more coffee on her way back.

She saw his shadow before she heard him. Her heart stopped. He was here. She reached out instinctively, flipped the on the light switch and stepped into the room. She kept her back to him while she fought for control of her emotions. She put the box down on a stack of empty boxes and turned around. He filled the doorway.

She couldn't speak as if God, Himself, had shut her mouth.

He looked better than she remembered. His amber eyes caught her and held.

"Erica."

Her tongue loosened enough to say, "Was it you?"

"Aldred?"

She shook her head, still not able to speak. His words had been with her these past weeks as she had re-read each of his books, but it was the last one that had the most effect. Aldred's path from a man of vice to a man of virtue was profound.

"Yes, well, mostly. He is a composite, but the essence is my journey."

She stepped closer. "I'm sorry I misjudged you."

"No need," he reached for her. She reached back.

He kissed her softly, sweetly. When he pulled back she rested her forehead on his shoulder.

"I met Ben ten years ago. I met Jesus eight years ago. I didn't struggle with my new life until I met you." His deep voice resonated from his chest into her. "For a year, I struggled so much that I put aside the book I'd just outlined and researched. I had to write this one instead. I didn't know why until you came. Then I knew. I wrote it for you."

"Me?" she choked out. He shook his head. That's why it had such a profound effect on her, so much so that she couldn't speak of it.

"I have something else for you." He pulled away from her, yet she didn't feel cut away as she had before. Instead the warmth between them spanned the room. He picked up a rectangular package wrapped in brown paper leaning against the wall by the door.

"Merry Christmas, Erica."

She took the package. Could it be? A painting? Was it the fox that had looked at her in his workshop? Maybe one of the haunting trees?

She peeled back the paper.

Her own eyes looked back at her.

Her heart overflowed at her eyes.

He only painted people he loved.

"Merry Christmas, Erica."

"You love me?" She blinked up at him.

"Yes. And I want to spend the rest of my life with just you."

###

Thank you for reading *The Christmas Gift.*

I hope you enjoyed meeting Jack and Erica. If you did, won't you please take a moment to leave a review at your favorite retailer?

Thanks, Iz

Discover other titles by Izzy James

Finding Boaz

I'd be delighted to hear from you:

Website: echull.com

Subscribe to my blog:

http://www.enotsilent.wordpress.com

Find me on Facebook:

https://www.facebook.com/IzzyJamesAuthor/

Favorite me at Smashwords:

http://www.smashwords.com/profile/view/izzyjames

#

A bonus excerpt from *Finding Boaz*...

"It's ten o'clock at night. What do you want?"

Abby Ericksen was looking through the screened door at her ex-husband Brad. His breath was fogging up the glass in the top of the door. The cold March air swirled past her knees through the screen in the bottom of the door and began to freeze her tiny cube of an apartment.

There goes the budget, she thought.

"Won't you let me in?" he pleaded. He never did like the cold.

"Where's Suzie?" The door stayed locked between them.

"She left me. Please let me in. It's cold out here."

"What do you mean 'left?'" Ordinarily she would have let a poor body in from the cold, but this particular body had left her and Chloe out in the cold when he left them for Suzie. So she would worry about the electric bill later. He could freeze.

"I just wanted to talk to you." He rested his arm on the doorjamb and leaned in as if there were no glass between them. The fog got worse.

"I just want to do the right thing here." He stepped away from the door and put his hands in the pockets of his jacket.

Her heart was banging as she opened the door. She used to dream of him coming back to her and Chloe. It was all so romantic in her fantasy: Brad arriving home in the middle of the night, ragged and torn from the violent struggle that it took to get back; sweeping her off her feet; finally carrying her away to

Neverland or some such place. But that was a year and a half ago, and she had given up those kinds of dreams.

Now that he was actually here, all she felt was anger and distrust. He stepped inside and leaned against the counter next to the back door. There were no signs of struggle. His blue Izod was completely intact under a black leather jacket that made her blue jeans and grandfather's old dress shirt feel frumpy.

Well, the time away from her had been prosperous for him anyway, she thought.

Crossing the ten-foot room, Abby backed up to the counter and got as far away from him as possible.

"I miss you, Ab, and I miss Chloe. I believe that we should be together. It's the right thing to do, don't you think?"

"I think you have a lotta nerve showing up here at my house in the middle of the night unannounced when I haven't seen you in eighteen months. That's what I think. So, what do you mean she left?" She crossed her arms over her chest.

"Can we stop talking about Suzie for a minute?"

"Don't you think she's relevant?"

"God allows these things for a reason, Ab, and I think that maybe we should just, you know, accept it." He opened his arms wide and started for her side of the room.

Abby sidestepped to the sink to clean up the tea glass she had sitting in it. What had he ever done but tout "what God said" and do the opposite? He came up behind her and put his hands on her waist. She felt giddy, like she might laugh, but it wasn't joy. Something wasn't right.

"Don't," She pushed him away.

He leaned against the counter next to her.

Stay in control, she thought. Abby turned to face him again. Beyond him she saw Chloe walk into the room.

"Momma?" Chloe's voice cracked with sleep. Brad turned in time to see her eyes widen.

"Daddy!" She ran and jumped into his arms.

"Hello, Chloe." Brad picked her up and held her close, but his eyes never left Abby. He sat down in a chair with the child on his lap. Chloe sat there quietly, almost sleeping. Abby leaned back against the sink with crossed armed. Maybe he was sincere. If so, it was the first time in at least eighteen months, although the timeline of his betrayal was much longer than that. Just then a brown spider scurried across the counter. She grabbed a paper towel and cleaned away the intruder.

"OK, Chloe, it's time to go back to bed." Abby retrieved her baby from his arms and carried her back to her room. She pulled the covers over the three-year old tucking them around her tightly.

"Is Daddy staying with us Momma?" Brad's eyes looked at her from the small face of her daughter.

"No."

When she returned, Brad was still sitting at the table. Abby took a seat across from him.

"What's all this?" He picked up one of the flyers lying amidst of an organizational reorganization in the middle of the table. "Old Thyme Festival? So you're still into that music thing, huh?" His mouth curled into a smirk.

"Yep." She straightened the piles into two stacks and drew them to her side of the table.

"I wonder how you have time to do that and work and take good care of Chloe," he said.

"Oh, Chloe loved it."

"So you brought her with you?"

"Of course–Mom came to help. She had a blast." He was doing it again, insinuating that she wasn't good enough. Anger surged as she realized she was reacting in the same old way she always did with him--always explaining, trying to justify herself to him.

"Well, what do you think?" he asked.

"About what?"

"Do you want to give it another try? For Chloe's sake?" His eyes were pleading.

"I have to think about it," she said aloud, surprised to hear herself say anything that would give him the slightest hope.

He pulled out a business card with his name imprinted on one side; on the other side he had written in the phone numbers of the hotel where he was staying and handed it to her. Abby took the card and laid it on the table between them. She had forgotten what ugly hands he had. They were too small and white; delicate like a woman's.

"This is where I'll be. I'm transferring here. I'll be here for two weeks looking for a place to live. Would you like to have dinner tomorrow night?"

"I don't know. I have to think about it," she looked away from his gaze.

"About dinner? You have to think about dinner?" He made a little laugh as his mouth curled into that smirk again, "Look, I just want to take you and my little girl out for a meal, OK?"

"It's probably OK. Just call me tomorrow."

As soon as he was gone, she threw all the locks on the door and sat back down in her chair exhausted.

He wants me back?

There was no question about that. The mere

thought made her sick. I should have just said "no."
She swiped her hand into the air, a gesture of finality.
"No."

Frustrated, Abby marched up and down the short
length of the room. What about Choe?

"How could he just show up here out of the blue
like that?" she asked aloud.

The room was silent. Her dulcimer stood on its
stand in the corner of the small living room. She
closed Chloe's door and sat on the couch to play.
Perhaps then she could sort out what she should do
next.

The dulcimer sat comfortably in her lap. She put
her music aside thinking to play unaided and free. At
first she couldn't feel any rhythm, but after a few
minutes, music began to fill the air. Her soul pulsed in
time with the music she made, and it soothed her
rattled nerves. She floated freely from one song to the
next losing her worries to the phrases and refrains as
she sang.

"Tom Dooley"...she had been playing "Tom
Dooley" the day she first thought something was
going on between Brad and Suzie.

The sun had been high and hot on the Fourth of
July two years ago. Neighbors and friends had turned
out for the annual block party. That year the buzz
question had been whether or not Eddy Mullen would
shoot a bottle rocket into a cop car as he had done the
year before. Abby had been jamming with Joe Smith
and his wife Joan on a makeshift stage on the
Mullen's front porch. Brad carried Chloe on his hip
making tours of the food tables. Generally Abby kept
her eyes down on the fretboard or on her music when
she was playing. If she didn't she couldn't go very fast
and Joe was lightning on the banjo. But she knew

"Tom Dooley" inside and out, and she was feeling free and easy, no pressure, just playing with friends. When she looked up, she saw Brad hand Suzie something. Suzie wrapped her hands around his as she took whatever it was from him.

Abby looked down quickly. She couldn't hear the music, and she wasn't sure where she was in the piece. It took a second to realize she hadn't stumbled; her hands had kept the pace. She glanced once more to catch Suzie's look of triumph. Brad melted back into the crowd with Chloe.

"Poor boy, you're bound to die..."

She let the dulcimer ring the last notes until it rested quietly.

"Amazing grace! How sweet the sound."

Abby played the old song slowly, purely, letting the lonesome sound resonate.

Two days later, Brad was gone. Near as she could figure, the "something" she had seen was a set of keys and a lease. He and Suzie moved into an apartment across town and wouldn't tell her where. Brad came to see Chloe a couple of times, but Abby never saw Suzie again. Perhaps she was hiding out, ashamed to show her treacherous face to her friend.

After they were divorced and sold the house, Abby moved to Ocean View, not because she grew up there, but because it was where her mother lived. Abby had not realized that she missed the sea until she moved back within sight of its shores. The ever-present bigness of it had always helped her keep perspective on the size of her own troubles, and the constant splash and roar of the waves brought solace.

As Ocean View had grown to be her home, her mother had grown to be her friend.

There had been so many battles when she was

younger, a whole five years ago she chuckled to herself.

"'Tis grace that brought me safe this far..."

Her mother had been opposed to everything that Abby had tried after high school. When she found the Lord and a church, her mother had violently protested. So when Helen hadn't liked Brad, Abby wasn't surprised. She had attributed her mother's resistance to Brad as part of her general cynicism and overall dislike of people as a rule. Abby now understood that as an emergency room nurse, Helen had seen a lot of the bad side of humanity, and as a result, she had come to expect the worst of everyone.

At the time, Abby hadn't understood her mother's concerns. Abby saw the world through new eyes, and trusted everything and everyone. Her mother had been suspect of everything and everyone, and she had been so right.

The divorce had taken a full year to become final. The contact between her and Brad had been minimal. Chloe had never been an issue with him– Abby wanted her Abby could have her. Chloe would be better off that way, he said. It made this present offer even more strange. She wondered if it would have been different if Chloe had been a boy.

"Did you ever hear tell of Sweet Betsy from Pike, who crossed the wide prairies with her lover Ike?..." She played the old waltz quickly.

And now here he was.

She stopped playing.

She should just say, "No." Just no.

It would be so much easier to have help with Chloe, she argued with herself. Brad was her father after all; he should be helping with the child. It could be good for Chloe. She needed to have a father, and her own was probably the best bet to do a good job with her. And it would be so much easier to get by on more than just her income, which she thought wryly, she had no more as of today.

Imagine Stanley, her boss, a man at least thirty years older than her, thinking she'd take a boat ride with him, his friend, and a case of beer! Her stomach knotted as she remembered the twinkle in the older man's eye and the feel of his rough fingers on her forearm. She had said no, and walked out. Unemployed.

Could Brad be right? Did the Lord send him because of this present trouble? It wouldn't be the first time God had chosen an unbeliever to bring about His will.

Technically, Brad wasn't an unbeliever, she guessed, but he had gotten so good at manipulating the truth that she no longer knew if he really was saved. There had been a time when she was sure of it, but no more.

Abby began to play the waltz again. Well, what about Chloe, she asked herself. If he's decided to act like her father then it might be good for her. He can have visitation. She stopped short. Would he steal her?

Not likely. If he had wanted her so badly, why would he have dumped her in the first place and not seen her in eighteen months?

She began to play again.

I just won't let him see her alone. If he wants to see her, he'll just have to see me too.

Her thoughts turned to her interview on Monday. Perhaps that was what God had in store for them next. The idea of working for a company of charter boats intrigued her. There was romance in the thought of pirate ships and being free on the waves in the light of the moon, the friendly beacons of lighthouses and brisk breezes . . . .

Right, I'll likely freeze my knees. She laughed.

Of course, it might just be great.

"And Betsy, well satisfied, said with a shout, 'Good-by, you big lummox, I'm glad you backed out.'"

Abby finished the song with a flourish. After she returned the dulcimer to its stand, she stood and stretched. The peace she felt radiated to her fingers and toes, she was ready for bed.

All that was left was to tell Brad.

35252503R00059 .

Made in the USA
Middletown, DE
26 September 2016